HJ

For my
Royal Party,
one wishes
to invite

....

1st

Peppa Pig™

LADYBIRD BOOKS

UK | USA | Canada | Ireland | Australia | India | New Zealand | South Africa

Ladybird Books is part of the Penguin Random House group of companies
whose addresses can be found at global.penguinrandomhouse.com.

www.penguin.co.uk   www.puffin.co.uk   www.ladybird.co.uk

Penguin
Random House
UK

First published 2022
001

Licensed by
Hasbro   eOne

Printed in China

The authorized representative in the EEA is Penguin Random House Ireland,
Morrison Chambers, 32 Nassau Street, Dublin D02 YH68

A CIP catalogue record for this book is available from the British Library

ISBN: 978-0-241-54342-9

All correspondence to:
Ladybird Books, Penguin Random House Children's
One Embassy Gardens, 8 Viaduct Gardens, London SW11 7BW

FSC
www.fsc.org

MIX
Paper from
responsible sources
FSC® C018179

Peppa's Royal Party

Peppa and her family were very excited when Mr Zebra the postman arrived with a special letter.
"This is for you, Mummy Pig," he said. "It has a crown on it. I think it must be from the Queen."

Mummy Pig opened the envelope very carefully.
"What does it say?" cried Peppa.

"It's an invitation," said Mummy Pig. "The Queen
is giving me an award for the book I wrote.
She has invited us and our friends to her
Platinum Jubilee garden party."
"Oooh, goody!" said Peppa. "What's a
plat-i-mum joo-bee-jee party?"

"It's a special party
to celebrate the Queen
having been queen for
seventy years," explained
Daddy Pig.
"Wow!" gasped Peppa.
"She must be nearly as
old as you, Daddy!"
Daddy Pig chuckled.
"Almost," he said.

Peppa phoned her friends to invite them to the Queen's party . . .

"There will be lots of guests," Peppa told Rebecca Rabbit.

"I'll ask my mummy to pack a GIANT picnic!" said Rebecca.

"The Queen has a BIG garden," Peppa told Suzy Sheep. "We should take some games to play!"
"Yippee!" cried Suzy. "I'll do that!"

"What should I wear?" asked Danny Dog.
"Your smartest clothes," said Peppa. "And bring boots for jumping in puddles."

"I know just what to pack . . ." said Freddy Fox.

The Queen sent a big red bus to take
everyone to the palace.
"Are you sure we need all these bags?"
asked Daddy Pig.
"We can't turn up to a royal party without
bringing anything," said Mummy Pig.
"That'd be rude."
"Ho! Ho! Very true!" said Daddy Pig.
"We wouldn't want to be rude."

Peppa and her friends made up a song on their way to the palace. They sang it very loudly . . .

"It's the royal party today,
Let's sing all the way!
It's the royal party today,
Hip hip . . . HOORAY!"

Hee! Hee!

Hee!

As the bus got closer to the palace, there were lots of people setting up their own garden parties for the Queen's jubilee. Peppa and her friends tried to do special little royal waves.

"Lots of people are celebrating with the Queen today!" said Daddy Pig.

When they arrived at the palace, everyone was very excited.

"I think there will be a giant chocolate fountain!" whispered Suzy.
"Seventy giant chocolate fountains!" said Freddy.
"I think she will have an enormous gold cake!" whispered Peppa.
"Seventy enormous gold cakes!" said Freddy.

The doors opened, and they were led out to the palace gardens.
They were surprised to see . . .

. . . no food or drinks or games!

"Oh, erm, hello there," said the Queen. "Thank you for coming.
I'm afraid we've had a slight . . . hiccup."

"Sorry to hear you have hiccups, Your Majesty," said Peppa.

"No, I'm quite all right," replied the Queen. "It's my party planner. He got the date muddled up. He thought the jubilee was tomorrow, so we cannot have my party today!"

Everyone gasped.
"But you *must* have your party, Your Majesty!" said Peppa.

Oh
no!

"Must I?" asked the Queen.

"Oh, yes!" said Peppa. "The whole country is waiting to celebrate with you."

"I'm not sure I can," said the Queen. "I don't have any party things."

"We've brought some with us. What do you need?" asked Peppa.

"That's very kind, but we need an awful lot," said the Queen. "Food for all the guests . . ."

"My mummy sent this picnic for everyone," said Rebecca, unpacking a GIANT picnic, with plates of cakes, sandwiches and jellies.

"My dad packed me these teapots and chairs," said Freddy. "They're made of real fake gold!"

"This picnic looks wonderful," said the Queen. "But what will we do other than eat and drink? I don't have any games." "I have these, Your Majesty," said Suzy, who had three big boxes of garden games. "Will they be OK?"

"What fun!" said the Queen.
"Yes, they will do quite nicely!"

Peppa and her friends pulled out balloons, bunting and even a music box from their bags. Soon the garden was transformed into a royal party fit for a queen!
"How extraordinary!" said the Queen. "You have brought everything one needs for a royal party."

"You could say we pulled it out of
the bag, Ma'am!" said Daddy Pig.

When the other guests started to arrive, they were very impressed.
"It looks wonderful!" they said. "This is the best jubilee ever!"

The Queen presented Mummy Pig with her award, then everyone tucked into the picnic. But as they finished eating . . .
Pitter, patter!
"Oh no!" gasped the Queen. "I believe it's raining. Whatever shall we do?"
"Don't worry," said Peppa. "I've got an idea!"

Peppa whipped out a pair of boots with a crown on them and pointed at a muddy puddle. "I brought a spare pair of boots for you, Your Majesty!"

"How delightful, Peppa!" said the Queen. "I dare say a royal party is not a royal party without some muddy-puddle jumping!"

"Three cheers for the Queen . . . and Peppa!" everyone cried.

Hip hip hooray!

Hip hip hooray!

Hip hip hooray!

That evening, everyone sat down to watch the Queen
make a speech.
"I would like to thank Peppa Pig," said the Queen. "Without
her help, my Platinum Jubilee would not have gone ahead.
I am giving her the Queen's Award for Royal Party Planning!"
"One does love a royal party!" said Mummy Pig.

Everyone loves a royal party!